T.L.C.

Written by:
M.H. Clark

Illustrated by:
Shahab Shamshirsaz

"Mom!" I said when I came home. "Come play with me!"

"Oh, sweetie," Mom said, "I'm too tired.
I could really use a little T.L.C."

T.L.C., I thought, T.L.C.
I don't know what that is,
but I'm going to get it for her.

I cracked and I measured.
I squeezed and I zested.
I whisked and I whipped.
And finally, my T.L.C. was complete!

"Ta-da!" I said, "One deeeeelicious Tart Lemon Custard!"

"Thanks, sweetie," Mom said.
But she didn't open her eyes.

Oh no, I thought.
T.L.C. must be something else.

I thought
and I thought.

I was full of good ideas!

I made a phone call. I made another.
Mom had lots of T.L.C. coming her way.

"Look, Mom,"
I said as I opened
the door,
"T.L.C.!"

Tiny
Licking
Chihuahuas
ran into
the room.

They licked my mom. They licked each other. They licked me.
They rolled in the custard. They got custard paw prints everywhere.

"Sweetheart," Mom said, "that's not quite what I had in mind..."

In came a woman with a very big box. She opened it.
A bright cloud of something flew out.
"Mom! A Tropical Ladybug Collection!"

But my mom shook her head.

So I opened the door.

In came a Tie-dyed Llama, Cartwheeling.
The llama flipped over and over, faster and faster.

My mom looked upset. Maybe she wanted something friendlier.

So I opened the door.

In slumped a Timid Lavender Creature.
It was ten feet high and covered in fur. I couldn't see its eyes.

The creature sat down next to my mom. It patted her knee.
But she didn't look any happier. Actually, she looked a little scared.

So I opened the door.

Some Trombone-Loving Clowns came in. They started to play.
The lavender creature tapped its toes. The llama listened.
The ladybugs flew everywhere. The lobster catcher stood still
and watched. The Chihuahuas licked. And I danced and I danced.

But Mom didn't seem
to like the music.

So I opened the door.

In came a Trapezing Lemur Circus. They
set up their trapezes without a peep, then
they hung and they swung and they flew overhead.

I clapped and I clapped, but Mom did not.

Just then, the wall shook. Everyone watched as the back end of a truck broke through.

It beeped.

"A Truck of Liquid Chocolate!" I shouted as delicious warm chocolate made a huge puddle in the living room. I jumped in. I waded around.

And then, suddenly...

"Stop!" Mom yelled, "Stop!"

"I don't need Tart Lemon Custard," Mom said, "or
Tiny Licking Chihuahuas, or a
Tattooed Lobster Catcher, or a
Tropical Ladybug Collection, or a
Tie-dyed Llama Cartwheeling, or a
Timid Lavender Creature, or
Trombone-Loving Clowns, or a
Trapezing Lemur Circus...

And I certainly don't need a
Truck of Liquid Chocolate."

She looked at me very seriously.
"What I need is a little Tender Loving Care."

"Oh!" I said. "I can do that!"
I sat down on the couch and gave my mom a very big hug.

"That," said Mom, "is just what I needed."

"This Looks Crazy!"

COMPENDIUM®
live inspired.

WITH SPECIAL THANKS TO THE ENTIRE COMPENDIUM FAMILY.

CREDITS:
Written by: M.H. Clark
Illustrated by: Shahab Shamshirsaz
Edited by: Amelia Riedler
Creative Direction by: Julie Flahiff

Library of Congress Control Number: 2014943682
ISBN: 978-1-938298-42-4

1st printing. Printed in China with soy inks. CPSIA A0Z1411001